Do Fairies Bring the Spring?

May the fairies
always help your
gardens grow! Best, *[signature]*
2017

Liza Gardner Walsh

Illustrated by Hazel Mitchell

Down East Books

Camden, Maine • Guilford, Connecticut

To Carol, for always trusting that things will bloom.
—L. G. W.

In memory of Jane Holmes, who loved all growing things
and the fairies who brought them.
—H. M.

Published by Down East Books
An imprint of Globe Pequot
www.rowman.com

Distributed by NATIONAL BOOK NETWORK
800-462-6420

Text Copyright © 2017 by Liza Gardner Walsh
Illustration Copyright © 2017 by Hazel Mitchell

All rights reserved. No part of this book may be reproduced in any form or by any elec-
tronic or mechanical means, including information storage and retrieval systems, without
written permission from the publisher, except by a reviewer who may quote passages in a
review.

British Library Cataloguing in Publication Information Available

Library of Congress Control Number: 2016950111

Manufactured by Thomson-Shore, Dexter, MI (USA); RMA14HC000, December, 2016

ISBN 978-1-60893-633-5 (hardcover)
ISBN 978-1-60893-634-2 (e-book)

∞™The paper used in this publication meets the minimum requirements of
American National Standard for Information Sciences—Permanence of Paper
for Printed Library Materials, ANSI/NISO Z39.48-1992.

WHEN all the blossoms of spring begin to appear,
Do you think there might be fairies near?

Do the fairies pull out
all the stubborn shoots
and brush out winter's
tangled roots?

Are they huddled around in their fairy house towns,
planning on ways to fill the bare ground?

AFTER a long winter's rest with little to do,
are the fairies ready to start something new?

WILL the fairies put on their finest spring clothes—

party dresses and wings spritzed with rose?

AND as they dress up
do they coax all the color
while hiding shades
that are so much duller?

Do they use tiny brushes and oil pastels

to paint crocuses, lilacs, and daffodils?

OR do they ring jingly bells
and sing spring songs
to wake the plants
that have slept too long?

As the days get longer,
do they ever skip a beat
tap-tapping the ground
with their tiny feet?

DOES this pitter-pat wake
the natural world up
so we'll soon have
lovely flowers to pluck?

Or is it just chance that they grow side by side,
young fairies and plants on the same wild ride.

PERHAPS they rely on what each has to offer

both of their spirits making the other one softer.

FOR without the plants
would fairies cease to be?
And without fairies
would plants vanish entirely?

ALL we know is that they teach
the same tricks of the trade:
how to be patient and gentle,
quiet and brave.

So as bright petals open and spring blankets the land
can you imagine a fairy's little hand

helping things grow to make all of us smile
and reminding us to sit and enjoy nature a while?

WAYS to ENCOURAGE FAIRIES in the SPRING

One of the best ways to help fairies in the spring is to work in the garden, planting and tending to all the new growth. If you are gentle with your plants and kind to the tiny creatures who visit them, the fairies will return the favor by creating a healthy and flourishing garden. Certain flowers, such as bluebells, will bring fairies, while others, like phlox, yarrow, and honeysuckle, will attract their good friends, the butterflies and birds.

But there are other things besides planting that you can do to help the fairies bring the spring.

- ~MAKE A SIGN in your garden or yard to welcome the fairies.

- ~FEED THE BIRDS.

- ~PLANT MILKWEED to help feed monarch butterflies on their marathon migration.

- ~FIX UP FAIRY HOUSES that have been damaged by the winter.

- ~But the most important of all, is to LAUGH AND FROLIC in nature.

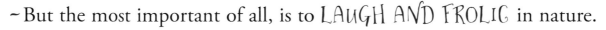